Curious George®

AT THE FIRE STATION

Adapted from the Curious George film series
edited by Margret Rey and Alan J. Shalleck

SCHOLASTIC INC.
New York Toronto London Auckland Sydney

ISBN 0-590-40432-6

Copyright © 1985 by Houghton Mifflin Company and Curgeo Agencies, Inc.
Adapted from the Curious George film series edited by Margret Rey and Alan J. Shalleck.
Reprinted by Permission of Houghton Mifflin Company.
All rights reserved. Published by Scholastic Inc.,
730 Broadway, New York, NY 10003,
by arrangement with Houghton Mifflin Company.

12 11   04 03
Printed in the U.S.A.

George and the man with the yellow hat
were visiting the fire station.

"Hello, George," said the fire chief. "How would you like to wear a fireman's hat?"

George put on the big hat.

Then they looked at the fire engines. "We're proud of them,"
said the chief. "We keep them as bright and shiny as we can."

One fireman was polishing a big brass bell on the wall.
"This is our alarm bell," said the chief.
"Whenever there is a fire it rings."

Another bell was on the engine.

"We ring that bell on our way to the fire," said the chief,
"so that people will get out of the way."

"And this is Sally, our Dalmatian. She just had ten puppies.
The puppies stay in a basket on the second floor with the firemen."

They all went up to the second floor. The puppies were in a
straw basket by the wall.

"Yip! Yip! Yip!" they barked. One tried to jump up and lick
George's face.

Near the basket was a big round hole with a pole in the middle.
"When the alarm rings," said the chief, "the firemen
slide down the pole to the fire engines below."

"You may slide down if you want, George," said the chief.
"But be careful!" said the man with the yellow hat.

George slid down the pole like a real
fireman.

Then he climbed onto the fire engine

and sat behind the steering wheel.

Make way, here comes George the fireman!

George was curious.
What would happen if he rang the bell?

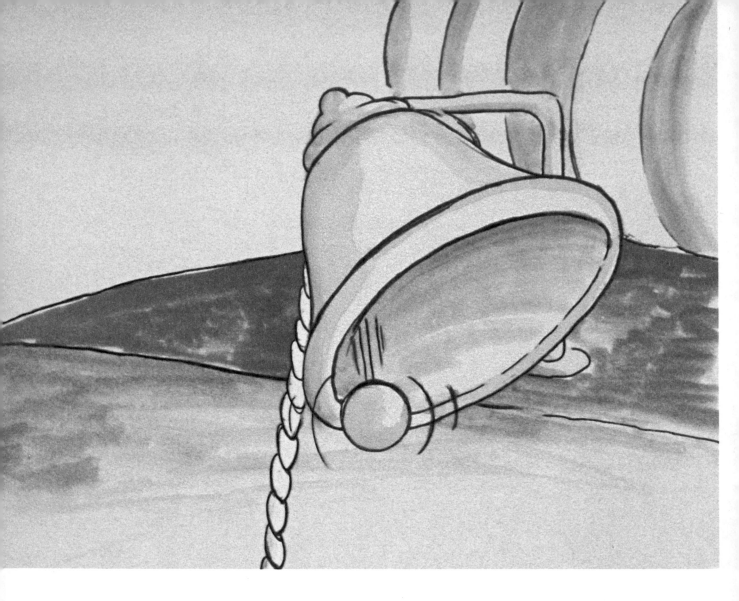

Clang! Clang! Clang!
went the bell.

The firemen heard it and jumped out of bed.

"Fire! Fire! Fire!" they shouted.

Quickly they put on their uniforms and slid down the pole.

It was a false alarm. When the firemen got to the engine
all they saw was a little monkey.

"George," said the chief, "fighting fires is serious business.
Get off that engine right now!"
George felt terrible.

At that moment, they heard a dog bark. Sally was
looking up to the top of the fire pole.

One of the puppies had gotten out of its basket
and was looking over the edge of the hole.
One more step and it would fall.

George knew what to do. He climbed up the pole as fast
as he could.

Then he held out his hat to catch the puppy in case it should fall. Sure enough, the puppy slipped and—

plop!—landed right in George's hat.

"That was using your head, George," said the chief.
"You saved the puppy. I'm making you an honorary fireman
of our station. You can keep the hat, too."

"Come back to visit us anytime," shouted the chief,
as George and the man in the yellow hat got into their car
to drive home.